THE TOSSY-TURNY PRINCESS
AND THE PESKY PEA

A Fairy Tale to Help You Fall Asleep

words by
SUSAN VERDE

pictures by
JAY FLECK

Abrams Books for Young Readers
New York

For my Josh,
always my partner in insomnia
—S. V.

To Audrey
—J. F.

The illustrations for this book were made in pencil and colored digitally.

Library of Congress Cataloging-in-Publication Data
Names: Verde, Susan, author. | Fleck, Jay, illustrator. Title: The tossy-turny princess and
the pesky pea : a fairy tale to help you fall asleep / words by Susan Verde ; pictures by Jay Fleck.
Description: New York : Abrams Books for Young Readers, 2021. | Audience: Ages 4 to 8. | Summary: After a pea
accidentally gets between her mattresses, a busy princess has trouble falling asleep but with help from the
gardener, cook, librarian, and astronomer she learns to relax her mind and body. Includes directions for a yoga
and meditation bedtime routine. Identifiers: LCCN 2020011305 | ISBN 9781419745874 (hardcover)
Subjects: CYAC: Insomnia--Fiction. | Princesses--Fiction. | Relaxation--Fiction. | Bedtime--Fiction. | Animals--Fiction.
Classification: LCC PZ7.1.V46 Tos 2021 | DDC [E]--dc23 LC record available at https://lccn.loc.gov/2020011305

Printed and bound in China
10 9 8 7 6 5 4 3 2 1

Abrams Books for Young Readers are available at special
discounts when purchased in quantity for premiums and promotions
as well as fundraising or educational use. Special editions can also be created to specification.
For details, contact specialsales@abramsbooks.com or the address below.

Abrams® is a registered trademark of Harry N. Abrams, Inc.

ABRAMS The Art of Books
195 Broadway, New York, NY 10007
abramsbooks.com

Once upon a time there was a princess who loved to sleep.

It helped that her bed was piled high with the softest mattresses, the coziest blankets, and the fluffiest pillows. But what the princess loved *most* about sleeping was that it gave her the energy she needed to go through her day with joy and attention.

This was important, because the princess had a very busy schedule!

Her first stop in the morning was always the garden.

She loved to help the royal gardener pull weeds,

smell flowers,

watch tiny creatures scuttle around in the grass—

and of course, try new vegetables. (Her favorites were the peas!)

Then she visited the royal chef in the kitchen. The royal chef always let the princess help her with the baking and cooking. The princess was a pro at whisking eggs—and tasting sweet desserts!

Next, the princess stopped by the library. The royal librarian always knew the perfect book to share with her.

Sometimes he read out loud, and the princess hung on every word, asking questions when she didn't understand.

And when the sun set, the princess visited the
royal astronomer. Together they climbed the highest tree
to get a look at the stars in the night sky.

The astronomer would tell her about the
planets, the constellations, and the meaning

At the end of such a long and wonderful day, you can imagine that the princess was ready to sleep so she could do it all again in the morning.

But tonight, there was a problem.

You see, earlier in the day while the princess was out, the prince was poking around in her room to borrow his favorite book of fairytales.

At the same time, he was eating his lunch . . .

a big bowl of fresh
         pea
              soup.

Suddenly, one of the big fresh peas rolled off of his spoon and fell right in between the princess's mattresses! UH-OH!

The prince tried to reach it, but it had rolled too far in. So he left the pea, figuring the princess would never notice, anyway.

Oh, how he was wrong!

That night, the princess got ready for bed, excited to hit the hay.
She climbed atop her many mattresses, got under her soft sheets
and cozy blankets, and laid her head on her fluffy pillow.

But she didn't feel right.

She felt . . . uneven, out of sorts, off balance.
As if something was poking her.

She tossed

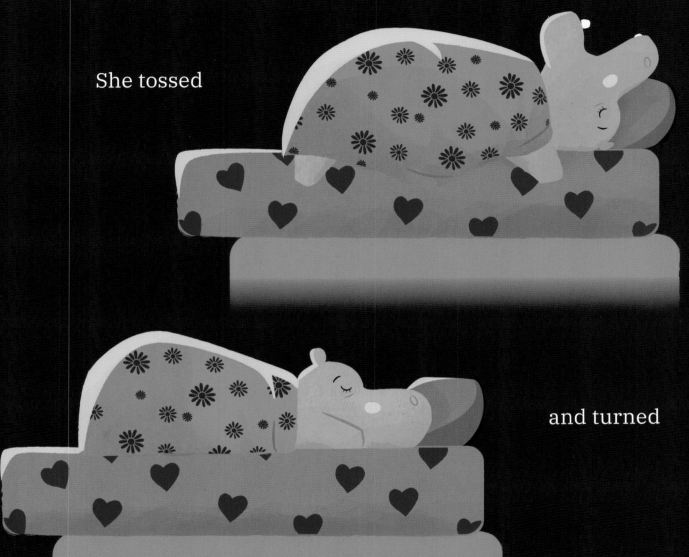

and turned

and tried to get comfortable,
but nothing was working.

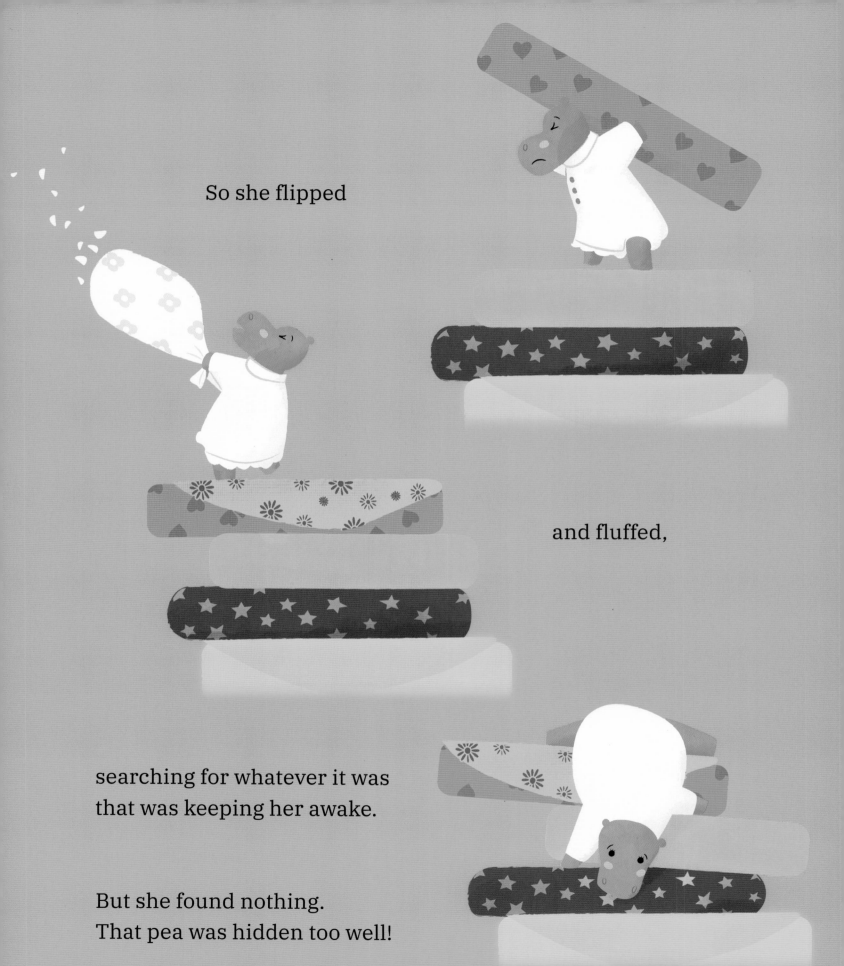

So she flipped

and fluffed,

searching for whatever it was
that was keeping her awake.

But she found nothing.
That pea was hidden too well!

Now the princess was wide awake.
And she stayed that way
all

night

long.

The next day, nothing went right.

The princess was cranky and clumsy, and she found herself dozing off in all sorts of places.

That night was even *worse*. Her head was filled with worries.

What if she felt the same thing poking her?

What if she was up all night?

What if she couldn't bake or garden or do any of the
things she loved because she was too tired?

What if she could never sleep again?

And once more she was up all night.

The next morning, she wearily went to visit the garden and promptly laid her head on the cool soil. The royal gardener asked, "What's wrong, princess?"

"I can't seem to fall asleep at night."

"You know," he replied, "when I have trouble sleeping, I make my body into the shape of the lizards I see in the garden. That always makes me sleepy."

In the kitchen, the princess dozed off while she was in the middle of whisking some delicious icing. The royal chef asked, "What's wrong, princess?"

"I can't seem to fall asleep at night."

"You know," she replied, "when I have trouble sleeping, I breathe in and out slowly through my nose, like I'm smelling the most delicious cookies coming out of the oven. That gets my energy out and makes me sleepy."

The princess managed to get herself to the library—but she fell asleep with her face in a book. "What's wrong, princess?" asked the royal librarian.

"I can't seem to fall asleep at night."

"You know," he replied, "when I have trouble sleeping, I flip onto my back and put my legs up against the bookshelves, like this. It makes me very drowsy."

By the time she reached the climbing tree, the princess was so exhausted she could only sit and lean against it.

The royal astronomer sat on the ground next to her. "It seems you're having trouble sleeping, princess. When that happens to me, I like to lie down, let my whole body relax, and look up at the sky. Then I place each of my worries on a star, until with every sparkle, they disappear. This helps my mind get quiet to make room for dreams."

That night, when the princess found herself wide awake once again, she remembered what her royal friends had shared that day.

It seemed they all had trouble sleeping sometimes. It felt a little better to know she wasn't the only one.

And they each did something special that helped. The princess thought that maybe if she did what they did, it might help her too.

So she got out of bed, and she stretched like the lizards in the garden until her legs felt longer and the wiggles started to leave her body. This made the princess feel calmer and a little more still.

Next the princess breathed in deeply through her nose, pretending to smell her favorite cookies like the royal chef. Soon she was feeling warm and peaceful.

Then, thinking of the librarian, the princess laid down on her back and leaned her legs up against the wall. It was so nice. She began to feel heavy and drowsy.

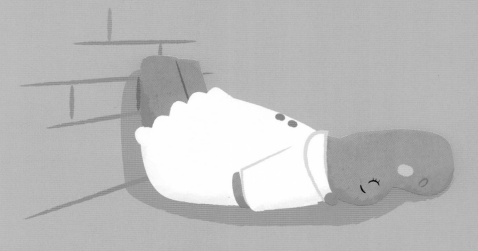

Soon the princess was sleepy enough to get into her bed. She climbed to the top of her stack of soft mattresses, got under her cozy blankets, and put her head on her fluffy pillows. She waited for that uncomfortable feeling to come back—but surprisingly, her body felt good and relaxed. It was her mind that was still filled with worries.

What if she still couldn't sleep?

What if she was too tired the next day?

What if . . .

Then the princess remembered what the astronomer had told her. Looking out her window, she saw the stars twinkling in the dark. She named all of her worries and sent each one to a star. With every twinkle, she imagined her worries disappearing into the night sky.

Before she knew it, the princess was sound asleep.

The next morning, the princess awoke fresh-faced and full of energy!

She couldn't wait to visit her friends and tell them how they had helped.

But as she climbed down from her bed, a large pea rolled out from between her mattresses and fell to the floor.

The prince, who had come to return her book, was standing in the doorway with a sheepish grin. "Oops! I think that was mine."

But the princess wasn't angry. In fact, she realized, it was the pea that had kept her awake—but it was also the pea that, along with her royal friends, had helped her learn how to fall asleep, even when she didn't think she could.

The princess gently picked up the pea and placed it in a very special spot right next to her bed.

When she saw it each night, she would remember that even when things didn't feel right—when her mind was worrying and her body was wiggling—she knew just what to do.

And *that* night, in celebration and in thanks, the princess threw a royal pajama party. Everyone practiced their nighttime poses and let go of all of their worries . . .

and the prince served
each guest a big bowl
of fresh pea soup!

AUTHOR'S NOTE

Just like the princess, we all have times when we can't sleep. Maybe something is making us physically uncomfortable (like a pea), maybe we feel wiggly instead of tired, or maybe our mind is busy worrying about big and little things.

In this story, the princess learns that there are things we can do to make falling asleep easier when we feel this way. Doing yoga and meditation before bed can help get out the wiggles and the worries. Sometimes it is nice to practice with a friend, a parent, or even a little brother as a bedtime routine. There are many good poses and exercises to get you sleepy—but here are the princess's favorites, which she learned from her helpful royal friends.

LIZARD POSE: Place your palms on the ground and reach your legs back behind you. Raise your bottom up and step your right foot outside your right pinky finger. Be sure your right knee is directly above your heel and not in front of it. If it feels like too big a stretch, gently lower your back knee to the ground, keep your chin lifted, and look ahead. Hold this pose for a few deep, slow breaths, then repeat using your other leg.

LINKING BREATH AND MOVEMENT: This is a way of slowing down your breathing and releasing extra energy from your body. Start with your arms hanging by your sides and begin breathing in through your nose very slowly. You can count to three or four if you'd like. Then breathe out for the same amount of time. Now add your arms: keeping them straight at your sides, lift them slowly up and over your head in time with your breath—1 . . . 2 . . . 3 . . . 4—and then slowly lower them as you breathe out. Do this for at least five rounds of breath. You can always keep going until you feel yourself getting calmer.

LEGS UP THE WALL: This pose is great for bedtime and relaxing! It helps you sleep, refreshes tired legs and feet, and helps with circulation, digestion, and any aches you might have. Start by sitting up against the wall sideways, with one hip and shoulder touching the wall. Next, lie down, turn toward the wall, and put your legs up against it. Try to get your bottom as close to the wall as possible and your back flat on the floor. You can always tuck a folded blanket under your head or lower back to feel as comfy as possible. Close your eyes and stay here for at least three to five minutes. You can always bend your knees a bit or do whatever else you might need to feel best in this position.

LET YOUR WORRIES GO: The princess gave each of her worries to the stars and imagined them disappearing with each sparkle. You can do the same. It can help to name your worries by saying them out loud, maybe to a parent or caregiver—or if it feels better, keep them to yourself and name them in your head. If there are no stars out or you aren't by a window, you can imagine your worries as pebbles. Think of each worry as a lovely pebble you are placing in a beautiful flowing river, and then watch them go downstream until they disappear. Make sure you take some deep, slow inhales and exhales through your nose as you do this. You will be amazed by how much better you feel when those big worries become smaller, leaving room in your mind for wonderful dreams.